The Mystery
Under Fugitive House

by Fredric Martin

Illustrated by James Teason

Little, Brown and Company

Boston · Toronto

to
Craig, Lee and Darin

LIBRARY OF CONGRESS CATALOG CARD NO. 67-19796

WEEKLY READER PAPERBACK BOOK CLUB
EDITION PUBLISHED BY ARRANGEMENT WITH
LITTLE, BROWN AND COMPANY

SECOND PRINTING, APRIL 1970

1

BANTAM BERNS heard a car below his second-story window, but he was too busy watching the planet Jupiter to bother to look down.

Through his high-powered telescope he could see the red spot on Jupiter just as clear as anything. Funny about that spot, he thought. It even puzzled astronomers. Some thought it might be a volcano exploding far under a layer of ice that covered the big planet. It was just a guess, though.

Jupiter's shape was changing, turning flat at the bottom, when the motor of the car died out. Bantam took his eye from the

telescope and glanced out of the window. The car's lights were out, and it was barely visible in the darkness.

Someone got out of it with a large, thin object about four feet square and carried it toward the basement door. Bantam wished that the moon were shining so that he could see whoever it was.

He sat and wondered if he should continue looking at Jupiter or go to bed. It was probably way past eleven o'clock and Aunt Janet didn't know he was up. She might have let him stay up if he had asked her. Then again, she might not have. He felt funny about it.

It would be a different matter if Uncle Dick was home, but he was working late. This was the first week they had lived here at Fugitive House, a large wood-framed inn on the shores of Moonbeam Lake in upper New York State. It was the only place Uncle Dick had been able to find that was close enough to his work. The inn not only had rooms for guests, but several apartments. Bantam was staying in one of them with his aunt and uncle until they found a house.

Uncle Dick was strict. Even more strict than Mom and Dad had been, or Miss Daley, his teacher back at Rock Island. And with good reason, too. No one but Bantam would dare bring a bumblebee into social study class in a glass jar and accidentally let it loose. No one but he would dare give Miss Daley a thirteen-inch baby alligator for Christmas, knowing that Miss Daley was even afraid of worms.

A movement outdoors caught Bantam's eye. The person was returning to the car empty-handed. A second later the car started up and headed for the road that ran parallel with the lake.

Bantam tilted the telescope to point in its direction and placed his eye to it. When the car reached the road, its headlights turned on. Just before the car turned left, Bantam spotted a red band running across the middle of the bumper, and the first part of its license plate, LF14. The car disappeared before he could read the other numbers.

Now what was that all about? Why did the person turn the car's headlights on *after* he had reached the road instead of before? Had he just forgotten to?

Bantam rubbed a fist across his tired eyes and brushed a lock of thick, black hair back from his forehead. He'd better go to bed. He didn't want to sleep too long in the morning, even though Aunt Janet and

8

Uncle Dick would let him. They had been very good to him since Mom and Dad died in an airplane crash over a year ago. They had no children of their own and were glad to take him under their wing.

But Bantam was always falling into mischief—whether he intended to or not.

A talking-to by the teacher, and then by the principal, had been followed by punishment from Mom and Dad. They would cut off his allowance for a while, or refuse to let him watch TV for a week, or forbid him to do something else he would like to do very much.

Sure, he'd promise not to get into trouble again. But somehow trouble would meet up with him, as if the two of them just couldn't stay apart for very long.

He had to try to avoid trouble as much as he could now that he was living with Aunt Janet and Uncle Dick. He couldn't—he just *couldn't*—let them get mad at him. Perhaps they would be sorry then that they had taken him in. And he loved them too much to ever be separated from them.

9

Just as he started to turn away from the window another movement caught his attention. A man had run out of the building and was heading for the road. He was slightly stoop-shouldered, and was carrying something under his left arm.

Bantam rose quickly from the stool to see where the man was going, and accidentally bumped the telescope with his elbow. The instrument spun off its perch on the tall box and crashed to the floor before he could catch it. The noise sounded like thunder.

Bantam froze. The telescope was the first instrument Aunt Janet and Uncle Dick had bought him. Stars and planets fascinated him. He had three books about them which he had read and reread.

Please don't let it be broken, he prayed. *Please.* Lenses were expensive, and his aunt and uncle had paid a lot of money for the telescope.

He stooped to pick it up and heard the door open. There stood Aunt Janet in her robe, staring at him. "What happened, Michael?" she whispered. Her eyes focused on the telescope in his hands. "Is that what made that noise?"

"Yes."

Aunt Janet closed the door behind her. The soft blue bulb in the lamp beside Bantam's bed heightened the look of curiosity on her face. "You shouldn't be up, Michael. Do you realize that it's after eleven o'clock?"

"It's a clear night," he said, avoiding her eyes. "I wanted to look at the stars and planets."

"You could have asked me," she said. "I might have let you."

Might have. She didn't say *would have.*

He looked at the lenses in the telescope. Thank goodness none were broken.

"Is it okay?" Aunt Janet asked.

"Yes."

He folded the legs of the telescope and put the instrument away in its cardboard box. Then he said his prayers and crawled into bed.

Aunt Janet pushed the stubborn lock of

hair back from his forehead and smiled. "Don't look so frightened. I'm not going to scalp you. But you did make me believe I could trust you, Michael."

"I'm sorry, Aunt Janet. You won't tell Uncle Dick, will you?"

"I'll tell him. But don't worry. He won't scalp you, either." She kissed him on the forehead. "Close your eyes and go to sleep."

"Aunt Janet." He rose to his elbow, his eyes suddenly wide. "A little while ago a car drove up and a man got out of it. He was carrying something. Then after he drove away, another man. . ." He faltered. He didn't want Aunt Janet to think he was afraid.

"Go on," she said curiously.

"This second man ran out of the building. He was carrying something, too."

"Sounds as if you saw a lot more than stars tonight. Did you recognize either one of the men?"

"No. It was too dark."

She pushed him gently back on the bed

and tugged the blanket up under his neck. "Forget it. They were probably men who work or live here. Fugitive House is a big inn. There are several families living here. Perhaps what you saw tonight happens all the time."

She switched off the light and went to the door. "Good night, dear," she said. "And sleep tight."

2

BANTAM pulled the covers up to his eyes. Aunt Janet had left the door open slightly so that the dim light in the hall shone in. What crazy things to be happening in the night. And it didn't make sense that they should happen all the time, as Aunt Janet had suggested.

The next morning he, Uncle Dick and Aunt Janet had breakfast together. Aunt Janet told her husband what Bantam had seen last night. He smiled as if it were nothing unusual.

"Don't worry about it, Bantam," he assured his nephew. "If something's wrong, Mr. Ward or one of his help will hear about it. We can tell them what you saw. Chances are the two men live here and were about their business."

An announcer was broadcasting the news over the radio. ". . . police are investigating a break-in at the Baker Art Museum in Brice, and the theft of one of the famous Von Rogen paintings which have been on exhibit. The painting, entitled *The Workers*, turned up missing this morning. Considered the most popular of all Von Rogen's works, the painting is valued at over a hundred thousand dollars."

"Wow!" said Bantam. "A hundred thousand dollars for a painting! Who'd give that much for a painting?"

"Art collectors," said Uncle Dick.

". . . the City Library Committee has announced the need for a larger and better-equipped library. . . ," continued the announcer.

Bantam brushed a napkin across his mouth, excused himself and left the table. A sound he had begun to hear earlier turned out to be what he had feared. Rain.

"Can I go out, Aunt Janet?" he asked. "I'll put my slicker on."

She smiled. "Okay. Better put your sneakers on, too."

"Where are you going?" asked Uncle Dick, resting back in his chair.

"By the lake."

"You still haven't met any young friends, have you?"

"No."

"Well, maybe you will." Uncle Dick squeezed his shoulder. "Just watch yourself, and don't be gone too long."

As Bantam walked out of the inn, he passed by the large dining room. Several people were in there eating.

"Well, hi, buddy," a voice halted him. "Going out in this rain?"

Bantam looked around at Melvin Sweeney, a waiter in the restaurant. Melvin was a tall young man with black, neatly combed hair. The long starched white apron he wore was spotless, as if he had just put it on.

Bantam nodded.

"Have you met that kid down the road?" Sweeney asked. "Kevin Wilson?"

"Not yet," said Bantam.

"You should. You know why?"

"Why?"

"His family's got water skis and a motor-boat. You'd like that, wouldn't you?"

Bantam laughed. "I sure would."

A tall, burly figure loomed in front of them. Bantam and Mel Sweeney cut their conversation short and looked at him. If anybody resembled a distant cousin to a bear it was Tony Torro, the restaurant manager.

"All right, Sweeney," he barked. "Don't you have anything to do but waste other people's time?"

"I'm just saying good morning," snorted Sweeney. "Is that against the law?"

"Gossiping about people ain't saying good morning," the big man grunted. He was taller than Sweeney and probably twice as heavy. His black curly hair and piercing black eyes made him look fierce, but Bantam knew that inside that barrel

17

chest of his was a big, kind heart. "You had a job to do. Go ahead and do it."

Sweeney jabbed a finger against Tony's stomach. "Yes, oh almighty El Torro," he said, and walked away.

Tony laughed, a deep-from-the-belly laugh. "He doesn't like my picking on him, that's why I do it," he said. "Well, how do you like it here?"

Bantam shrugged. "It's okay. Except there's not much to do."

"You'll find things to do, as soon as you get acquainted with the place. Take this building. It's old and famous. Know what it used to be over a hundred years ago? An underground railroad."

Bantam looked puzzled.

"No, not a regular railroad," laughed Tony. "And it didn't mean underground either. But in this case, I suppose, you can say it does. Fugitive slaves who had escaped from their masters in the South came up here to hide. That's how this building got its name. Fugitive House. There's a cave underneath here where they hid for days.

Then they'd take a boat and slip up north to Canada, or other parts of this country, hoping to find freedom and a new life."

"I didn't know that!" exclaimed Bantam. There must have been plenty of danger here back in those days.

He went outside into the rain. When he was close to the brink of the lake, he turned and looked at Fugitive House. Though he had lived in it for almost a week, he really had not paid much attention to it.

Tall, wood-framed and slate-roofed, with six gables pointing into the sky like steeples, Fugitive House was indeed one of the oldest buildings he had ever seen. There was a long porch in front, and two doors leading into the building. A garage was in the rear. To the right of Fugitive House was a beautiful, well-kept lawn, with a plum tree growing in the middle of it.

Fugitive slaves. The underground railroad. Thinking about the perilous things that had taken place here over a hundred years ago made Bantam's pulse tingle for a moment.

He walked to the edge of the lake and looked down at it some twenty-five feet below. Its wideness fascinated him. Rain marred its otherwise smooth surface. Ban-

tam picked up a stone and flung it, and watched the lake swallow it in a gulp.

A movement at his right drew his attention. About a hundred feet away, from a tiny shack nestled under a cluster of tall trees, a little old man approached. A slightly stooped old man with a stubble of whiskers on his chin, and a wide-brimmed straw hat that covered his long gray hair.

Bantam stared at him. Then, frightened, he turned and hurried toward Fugitive House. He stumbled over a jutting stone, fell, scrambled to his feet and went on as fast as he could.

The little old man looked like the figure he had seen last night stealing away from the building with something under his arm.

3

"WAIT! WAIT!"

Bantam was close to Fugitive House when he heard the new voice. He saw a boy and a girl running up from the road beside the lake. A half-dozen homes were strung far apart along both sides of the road, and the children probably belonged to one of them.

Bantam waited, still breathing hard from his flight. His right knee ached from the fall and he rubbed it.

The children came up to him, both smiling with wet faces. They wore hooded raincoats and boots.

"Hi," the boy said. "I'm Kevin Wilson and this is my sister Nancy. What did Old Farley do—scare you?"

Bantam nodded, and looked where he had last seen the old man. He was gone.

"He lives in that little old shack," said Kevin, pointing at a ramshackle building standing some sixty feet from the edge of the cliff overlooking the lake. "His name's Morton Farley."

"He's harmless," Nancy broke in, laughing. She looked about two years younger than her brother. "He scares me, too, just *looking* at him."

"I was throwing stones into the lake when I saw him," explained Bantam. "He was coming toward me."

"Maybe he wanted to meet you," said Kevin.

Bantam shrugged. "Well, I didn't want to meet him." He grinned then. "My name's Michael Berns. But I'm called Bantam."

They shook hands. "You live in the hotel?"

"Yes. We came here to Carr Point four days ago. Uncle Dick works at the gas and electric company and we're looking for a house."

"We live just beyond Old Farley's place," said Nancy. "It's a year-round cottage. Our dad works at the gas and electric company, too. He might know your uncle."

They walked up on the porch of the inn and sat down on old wicker chairs. "Old Farley looks like the person I saw sneaking away from here last night," said Bantam. "I'm not sure, because it was so dark. But the person I saw looked stooped, just like Old Farley is."

"Sneaking away?" Kevin peered at him, puzzled. "What do you mean?"

Bantam told them about seeing someone running out of Fugitive House with something under his arm. "He was running as if he had stolen it," he said. He didn't want to say anything about the car, or the person he'd seen coming out of it. No use bringing up a subject that could mean nothing. But the other figure—the stooped figure he had seen—he could almost swear it was Old Farley.

"I think you should tell Mr. Ward about it," said Nancy. "He owns Fugitive House, you know. He's gruff and all that, but he's okay."

"It's better to tell Mel Sweeney or Tony Torro," suggested Kevin. "Mr. Ward won't pay any attention to you. He thinks kids are brats. I'd like to know what he was like when he was a kid."

All at once Nancy jumped from her chair, excitement filling her eyes. "Kev, why don't we take Bantam to our cottage? He can meet Mom and Dad and Michelle and Polkie."

"Polkie?" Bantam grinned.

"His name's Jerome William Polk. We call him Polkie. Grandpa Polkie, but he's really our great-grandfather. He's ninety-one, but he's got a brain like a computing machine and reads without glasses."

Bantam laughed. "Just a minute. I'll ask my aunt and uncle. I'm sure they'll let me go."

They did, but with reservations. One: Remember to behave. Two: Return home in an hour.

The Wilsons' cottage was set some fifty

feet back from the cliff. A lawn, shrubbery and a white picket fence surrounding it gave it a comfortable, cozy look.

Michelle Wilson was a lot older than her brother Kev. She was starting college in September, Nancy told Bantam. "You'll meet her boyfriend, too," Nancy added. "Terry Lott. He's here most of. . . ."

"That, dear sister, is enough from you," Michelle interrupted, pointing a long, pink-nailed finger at her. But she was smiling, and Bantam couldn't help smiling, too.

Mrs. Wilson had baked molasses cookies—their delicious smell was all over the place—and she offered Bantam some. While he ate, he was introduced to Grandpa Polkie, a tall, bald man who walked with short, nervous steps. His voice was clear and his handshake strong.

"So you live in Fugitive House," he said, settling back into a high-backed rocking chair. "Anyone tell you that's a historical place?"

"Mr. Torro did," said Bantam.

"He offer to take you down into the cave sometime?"

"No."

"Didn't think so. None of them would. Manly Jones used to. He owned the place and sold it to Benjamin Ward. Ever since Ward had it he's put a lock on the basement door—the one leading into the cave, that is, and he keeps a rug over the other door—the trapdoor in the pantry. Well, maybe it's the right thing to do. People get pretty nosy and Ward's a man who can't stand nosy people." He ran a blue-veined hand across his bare head and smiled. "Someday I'll talk with that old codger and take you down into that cave myself."

Bantam smiled. "I'd like that," he said.

He played Chinese checkers with Kev and Nancy, then thanked them all for a pleasant time and walked back to the inn. He met Mel Sweeney in the hall and told him about seeing Old Farley going away from Fugitive House the night before with something under his arm.

"Old Farley?" Mel Sweeney frowned. "What time was that?"

"A little after eleven o'clock. I was looking at the stars and planets through my telescope."

"You sure it was Old Farley?"

"Pretty sure," said Bantam.

Sweeney tapped him on the shoulder. "Okay, Bantam. Thanks. I'll tell El Torro about it."

By afternoon the rain stopped. Bantam walked to the lake again, an eye out for Old Farley. He wasn't as scared of the old man now as he had been this morning. People were swimming in the lake in front of Kevin Wilson's cottage. Bantam recognized Kev and Nancy and Michelle and a young man who was probably Terry Lott, Michelle's boyfriend.

Bantam started for the cottage, glancing over his shoulder at the ramshackle house in which Old Farley lived. It looked only big enough for one room. A round stovepipe stuck out from the side and curved up into the air. A pile of kindling wood stood high against another side.

Poor Old Farley. All at once Bantam wished he hadn't said anything to Mel Sweeney. It didn't seem right that an old man should live all by himself in that shack. But maybe that's the way Old Farley wanted it.

Bantam walked on toward the cottage. A car was parked in front of it. It must be Terry Lott's. His eyes lowered to the license plate and suddenly he stared.

The first four figures on it were LF14. Not only that. A red band ran all the way across the middle of the bumper.

4

"BANTAM! Got a swimsuit? Come swimming with us!"

Kevin was at the top of the steps leading up from the lake. His white trunks were dripping wet and his body glistened with water beads.

"Yes. I've got a suit. But I—" LF14, he was thinking. Those were the first four figures he had read on the license plate of the car he had seen last night. Was it Terry who had taken something into the basement?

Kevin ran across the lawn toward him. "Come on. There's nobody here but us

Wilsons and Michelle's boyfriend, Terry. Ever water-ski?"

"Never."

"Then come on. Get your trunks."

Bantam forgot about the license plate and grinned. "Okay. Be right back." He ran as hard as he could all the way to Fugitive House, up the steps and inside and then up the long flight of steps to their apartment.

"Can I go water-skiing with Kev, Aunt Janet?" he blurted out. "They're all at the beach. The whole bunch of 'em. Can I, Aunt Janet? Where's Uncle Dick? You going somewhere?"

"Hold it. HOLD IT!" Aunt Janet raised up both hands. "Suppose you take a second breath and start all over again."

He inhaled deeply, exhaled, then started all over again.

"Don't you care about coming with us?" she said when he finished. "Uncle Dick and I are going house-hunting."

"Isn't it okay if I didn't go with you? Any house you and Uncle Dick pick is all right with me, Aunt Janet."

Uncle Dick walked into the room, buttoning his shirt. He chuckled. "Guess you and Kev have already hit it off," he said.

"Yes, we have. Can I, Uncle Dick? You really don't need me to go with you, do you?"

Uncle Dick laughed. "Well, it's okay by me," he said.

"Then it's unanimous," replied Aunt Janet. "But be home by five. Don't forget."

"Don't worry. I won't. Thanks, Uncle Dick. See you later!"

He grabbed his suit from the closet, plunged out the door and down the stairs, and suddenly wished he had given them each a kiss. Well, it was too late now.

His legs had never moved as fast as they did from the bottom step of Fugitive House down the road to Kev's house. Kev showed him into the kitchen where he changed into his suit. Then they walked down the steep flight of steps to the beach and Kev introduced him to Terry, a tall, blond young man whose wet, sunburned body was like polished bronze.

Bantam almost mentioned seeing Terry's car behind Fugitive House last night, but decided this was no time to talk about something that was no business of his in the first place.

He greeted Michelle, Nancy and Mrs. Wilson who were in the water, and then Grandpa Polkie, who was wearing trunks and dark glasses and reclining on a beach chair as if he were the kingpin.

"Howdy, neighbor," Grandpa Polkie greeted him. "You a good swimmer?"

"Pretty good," admitted Bantam. He ran onto the diving board and dove off, and suddenly knew that it was the poorest dive he had ever made. Plop! Right on his belly. The sting felt as if he had fallen onto a hot iron.

When he lifted his head above water, he heard Grandpa Polkie laughing hilariously. "Prettiest swan dive I've ever seen in my life!" the old man said.

Later Kev offered him a ride in their motorboat. Michelle rode up front with Terry, who piloted the craft. In the seat behind them Bantam sat with Kev and Nancy. They glided like a rocket over the water, the wind whipping against their faces and tangling their hair. As they rode in the middle of the lake past Fugitive House, Bantam saw a hole in the side of the cliff like the opened end of a huge barrel.

"Hey! That's the cave!" he cried.

"That's right," said Kev. "It runs under Fugitive House."

A narrow stream of water flowed from it and cascaded into the lake, shimmering like tinsel in the sun. The boat raced up the lake a mile or so, then made a wide turn and returned to the dock.

"Want to water-ski now?" Kev asked, smiling through the water beads on his sun-burned face.

"Sure!"

"Okay. Terry, mind driving the boat again? Bantam wants to water-ski."

"Okeydoke," replied Terry.

Minutes later Bantam was on the water-skis, gliding over the water behind the boat. An electric, breathtaking excitement rippled through him. He let his slightly bent knees give a little each time the skis bounced over a wave from the boat—*whoosh! whoosh!*—so he wouldn't lose his balance.

"Thataway, Bantam!" Kev shouted. "You're doing great!"

He grinned and took a hand off the rope handle to wave at Kev. The gesture made him almost lose his balance. Better keep both hands on it if he wanted to stay on the skis, he thought.

A few seconds later Terry began to turn the boat. Halfway around the turn, Bantam, trying hard to steer the skis with his weight, suddenly realized that he was leaning too far inward. He tried to correct his balance, but too late. He let the water-ski rope go and splashed into the lake. A few seconds later Terry pulled the motorboat up alongside of him and Nancy and Kev hauled him aboard.

"You did all right," said Kev, grinning. "A couple more times and you'll be an expert."

Bantam saw the others smiling at him. He wanted to shout his excitement at having ridden water skis for the first time, but he didn't. He'd hold it for later and tell it to Kev. They returned to the dock where Terry shut off the motor and secured the boat. Presently slow, heavy footsteps sounded and everyone looked toward the steps leading up to the Wilsons' house. Bantam felt his breath catch as he saw two state troopers, their bright leather holsters flashing in the sun. They reached the bottom step and came forward. "Whose car is that parked in front of the house?" the taller one asked.

"It's mine," said Terry.

The troopers looked at him. "What's your name?"

"Terry Lott." Terry's eyes were suddenly wide and worried. "What's up?"

"Better get dressed and come with us," the taller one said. "We have some questions to ask you."

5

WHILE Bantam changed into his clothes in the Wilsons' kitchen, he told Kev about having seen Terry's car in the rear of Fugitive House. "I spotted the first four figures of the license plate through my telescope," he explained. "That didn't really prove the car was his, because a lot of other cars might have the same first figures. But when the troopers picked him up I guess that proved it. What do you think he was carrying into the basement of Fugitive House in the middle of the night, Kev? Think that was why the troopers picked him up?"

Kev frowned. "It probably is. Seems as if

Terry had stolen something and hidden it in there. Guess someone else had spotted Terry's car, too, and reported it to the troopers." His eyes were glazed as he looked at Bantam. "I can't believe that Terry would steal anything, Bantam. He's not that kind of a guy. Anyway, what could he have stolen that he'd put in the basement of Fugitive House?"

"Something big and square. It was hard to see in the dark."

Just then there was a knock on the door. "Can I come in?" a voice shouted. It was Nancy.

"Oh-oh," said Kev. "Don't tell Nancy what you just told me about Terry's car. She'd tell Michelle and Michelle would get all shaken up. We'll talk about it later." He raised his voice. "Yes, you can come in!"

It rained again after supper. Bantam was unable to sit still in the apartment. All he could think about was the troopers picking up Terry. Had they arrested him? Had he committed a crime? What crime could he have committed, though? Had it something to do with whatever he had taken into the basement?

Thinking it over, Bantam wandered downstairs toward the lobby.

"Psst! Banty!"

Tony Torro was motioning to him from the kitchen. He went in, the delicious smell of hot rolls and bread, Harvard beets and a dozen other foods wafting across his nostrils and teasing his appetite, although he had left the supper table only a few minutes before.

"Banty, I want you should not say a word about what you saw last night," whispered Tony. "Understand? Mr. Ward hear about it and he'll fire me for sure."

"You mean about Old Farley?"

Tony's bearlike head bobbed. "Twice a week I fill up a bag with cooked meat and vegetables and set it just inside the back door for him to pick up. I've done it for months. Everybody knows about it—almost everybody, anyway—except Mr. Ward. Old Farley catches and eats a lot of fish, but a steady fish diet isn't real proper for no man. He's not a bad guy, Old Farley isn't. Was up to me I'd give him a room in this hotel and let him live like a human being should live. You saw that shack he lives in. It's an eyesore to the community. The only reason it stays up is because it's Old Farley's."

"Doesn't he have any relatives?" Bantam inquired.

"None at all. He used to live with his folks on the Lott farm, but he sold the place after they died and squandered the money on a trip around the world. Guess he was never too bright while he was young, and he certainly didn't get any brighter as he got older. People round these parts who knew his family felt sorry for him and put the shack up for him. But ten years ago it looked more respectable than it does today."

"Didn't anybody want to take him in?"

"Nobody." Tony leaned forward so close that a lock of his black hair brushed across Bantam's forehead. "The most likely person you'd think would help him would be

Mr. Ward. He's the richest around here. But you know what that ratty old skinflint said?"

Bantam shook his head no.

" 'The old bugger made his nest, let him sleep in it.' That's what he said. Now, I tell you, is that a thing to say . . ."

His heavy brows lifted, and his face suddenly paled. "Oh, hello, Mr. Ward. Me . . . me and Banty was just having a personal conversation."

"About what?" Mr. Ward snorted. He was standing in the doorway, a tall beanpole of a man with thick, black-rimmed glasses.

"Nothing in particular. Just talking." A warm grin spread over Tony's face as he looked at Bantam. "So long, Banty. Be talking with you again sometime." He stuck out a plump hand. Bantam put his into it, felt its gentle squeeze then started out, his skin prickling. If Mr. Ward had heard any bit of that conversation, it was the end of Tony Torro, for sure.

"Hi, Mr. Ward," he said, as he walked

toward the door blocked by the richest man in Carr Point.

"Hi," replied that worthy, making no move to get out of the way. "Looks to me like the two of you were talking about something real important."

"Well, yes, we were." Bantam felt the back of his neck bristle.

"Mind telling me what it was?"

Bantam turned large eyes toward Tony Torro, then looked back at Mr. Ward. "We were talking about you."

"About me?" Mr. Ward's eyes shifted suspiciously to Tony Torro, then returned. "Go on, Berns. What were you saying about me?"

"Oh, just that you owned Fugitive House, Mr. Ward. And that there's a cave underneath here that used to be an underground railroad during slavery days."

"Oh. Harumph. Well. Yes . . . yes, that's right." Mr. Ward frowned, as if the reply disappointed him, and gingerly stepped aside.

"Excuse me, Mr. Ward," said Bantam,

and walked by. Several seconds later he was dashing down the porch steps and waving to Kev who was running up the road.

"I was just coming to see you!" said Kev, panting.

"About Terry? Did the troopers bring him back?"

"Yes. But he's still their only suspect."

"Suspect?" Bantam frowned. "Did he really steal something?"

"Well, Terry says not. But the troopers said his car was the one parked outside an art museum last night. A valuable painting was stolen from it."

"Painting?" Bantam blinked. Where had he heard about a stolen painting? Suddenly he remembered. Over the radio! This morning while he and Aunt Janet and Uncle Dick were having breakfast!

"The caretaker at the museum happened to look out his window and noticed the car," Kev explained. "He got suspicious, but by the time he went downstairs the car was gone. But he had seen the license plate." Kev shook his head dismally.

"Terry swears he was home last night. He could prove it by his parents, he said."

Bantam's heart was jumping wildly. "Kev, got a minute?"

"Sure."

"Come with me."

Bantam led the way to the rim of Moonbeam Lake, the rain spattering in soft, whispery sounds against the hoods of their slickers.

"Where are we going?" Kev asked.

"Just be quiet. Let's go this way so that no one will guess we're up to any mischief."

"Mischief?"

"That's what my dad used to say every time I was going somewhere by myself. Mischief." He was usually right, too, Bantam admitted to himself.

They walked along the rim to their right, then cut back across the road to the rear of Fugitive House. At least the rain was a help, thought Bantam. It kept the grown-ups inside.

He hurried toward the basement door

that was near the middle of the building. About ten feet beyond was the door that led to the first floor, the door from which he had seen Old Farley run off with the bag of food Tony Torro had left for him.

"Kev, look!" exclaimed Bantam.

Lying on the wet ground was a brown calfskin glove! Bantam picked it up, shook the rain off as much as possible.

"It's too big for a kid's," observed Kev. "And it doesn't look like a woman's."

"Maybe the person dropped it last night when he got out of the car," guessed Bantam. "Maybe that's it, Kev!"

"But why would he be wearing gloves?"

"So he wouldn't leave fingerprints!"

"Stick it into your pocket," said Kev. "We'll try to find out later who owns it."

Bantam shoved the glove into his pocket, then the two boys descended the four concrete steps to the basement door. Bantam saw that only a four-inch piece of wood stuck into a latch kept it closed. It explained the quick entrance that Terry—or whoever it was—had made.

Quickly he removed the wood and pushed the door open. The daylight revealed a large room filled almost entirely with cardboard cases containing cans of food, and cases of empty and filled soda pop bottles. Another door was straight ahead. It was padlocked.

The boys wiped their rubbers on the burlap bag just inside the basement door.

"Think the painting's in here?" whispered Kev. "Think you saw Terry bring it in here?"

"I didn't say it was Terry!" said Bantam emphatically. "It was too dark to see who it was!" He paused then. "It isn't here."

"Maybe it wasn't the painting, Bantam."

"But it had to be!" Bantam looked at the padlocked door. Instantly the answer dawned on him. "That's where he took it, Kev! Through that door! Into the cave!"

6

THE padlock was a long, strong one. Bantam grabbed it and yanked it hard, hoping it might not be locked. It was.

"Who has the key for it?" asked Kev.

"Mr. Ward. He's the only one who has a key."

"He can't be."

"He is. Your grandfather Polkie said so."

"Then how could Terry have got in there —if it was him? He sure didn't bust in. And I don't think Mr. Ward would have lent him the key to hide a painting in there. Not the way Grandpa Polkie talks about him."

Bantam didn't know what to think. The police had proof that it was Terry's car that had been parked near the art museum, yet

Terry denied having gone out with the car that night. Had someone else taken the car, driven it to the art museum, stolen the painting, hidden it here somewhere, then returned the car? Would Mr. Ward do such a thing? *I can't believe he would*, thought Bantam. *I can't believe anyone would do a dirty thing like that.*

"Bantam, let's not make a peep about your seeing Terry's car here to anybody until we find out for sure what happened," Kev suggested. "If the painting's found in the cave and you tell the police you had seen Terry's car, they might stick him in jail for years and years. And that would be terrible, if he's innocent."

A bright object on the floor to the right of the door attracted Bantam. "Look!" he said. "A ballpoint pen!"

He picked it up. It was silver-colored, with the inscription: *Compliments of Fugitive House, Carr Point, N. Y.* "It's exactly like the one Mr. Ward gave us the day we registered at the inn," Bantam exclaimed in a low voice.

"So it must belong to someone who lives here!" said Kev. "Sh-h! Listen!"

There was a sound of a door closing. "Someone's coming!" whispered Bantam, sticking the pen into his raincoat pocket. "And the cellar door's open!"

"Let's hide!" breathed Kev.

They ran toward the darkest corner of the basement and hid behind a stack of cases. Someone came down the steps, paused a few seconds, then entered. Presently a case scraped across the top of another. A moment later the boys heard the person leave. Bantam stuck his head out just in time to get a glimpse of Mel Sweeney's back.

If he locks the door we're sunk, he thought.

An instant later Sweeney pulled the door shut behind him. The piece of wood that served as a lock was the sound of doom as the boys heard Sweeney drive it home.

"Murder!" said Bantam. "Now what're we going to do?"

The boys looked around the room. Two

small windows high on the wall and another small window on the farther wall provided plenty of daylight. And gave Bantam an idea.

"Let's pile up some cases in front of a window," he said, "and climb out through it."

"I was just going to say that," said Kev. Together they carried three cardboard cases containing canned food and piled them on top of each other below a window. Then Bantam climbed up, unlatched the window and crawled through. Kev followed him out and closed the window.

"Maybe we ought to put those cases back where they were," he suggested.

"Suppose Sweeney comes back for something and catches us? What'll we say to him?"

Kev sighed. "Let's forget the cases."

They heard a low, peculiar sound directly behind them and turned. Not five feet away was a green frog, its body half buried in a puddle of water.

Bantam picked it up, grinning. "The little

old buddy's lost," he said, and started talking to it.

"Think he knows what you're saying?" said Kev.

"Sure, he does. Can't you see how he listens?"

A window opened above their heads and Bantam saw Aunt Janet poke out her head. "Michael, don't you think you've been in that rain long enough? Come on in. You too, Kevin. And what's that in your hand, Michael?"

"A frog."

"A frog? Goodness gracious, a frog yet! Put it down and come inside!" She pulled her head back in and closed the window.

"Nobody has pity on a frog," said Bantam sadly. "Except me. Come on, froggie. You're coming in with us."

They went into the building, headed down the hall toward the staircase and met Sweeney coming out of the kitchen.

"Well, if it isn't Mike and Ike," Sweeney said, putting his hands on his hips. "Where have you guys been?"

"Outside," said Bantam. The frog uttered a weak croak and tried to jump out of his hand. Bantam tightened his hold on it.

"I didn't see you," said Sweeney. "I was out there just a few minutes ago."

"We saw you," said Bantam.

"Where were you?"

"Outside. You just didn't see us, that's all. You were busy going in and out of the basement."

The steps leading upstairs squeaked as someone started to come down. It was Mr. Ward, carrying a vase of flowers. Panic-stricken, Bantam stuck the frog into a pocket of his slicker. The owner of Fugitive House wasn't the type to allow even the most harmless reptile to breathe the air inside his building.

Mr. Ward stepped in front of Sweeney and the boys, and shot one of his glares at them. "What, again?" he snorted at Bantam. "Seems that every time I meet you, you're flabbergadding with one of my help."

"It sure seems like it, Mr. Ward," said

Bantam innocently. He took the glove out of his pocket. "We found this outside. Does it belong to one of you?"

"It's not mine," snorted Mr. Ward. "Who'd be wearing gloves in the summertime, anyway?"

"It isn't mine, either," said Sweeney.

Just then a sound came from Bantam's pocket and Mr. Ward's eyes switched on a grim, piercing light. "What was that? Sounded like a frog."

Bantam paled. You just couldn't hide anything from Mr. Ward. He put the glove back into his pocket and lifted out the frog. "You've got good ears, Mr. Ward. It is a—"

The frog jumped. Mr. Ward jumped, too, letting out a sharp squeal. But too late. The frog had disappeared into his vase.

"Sweeney! Here!" he yelled at the top of his voice. "Take this blasted thing outside and get that reptile out of it! Of all the maddest, wildest, craziest . . . ! Well, don't just stand there, you idiot! Take it!"

Sweeney took the vase and carried it

hastily toward the back door. It was a good time, Bantam thought, to make tracks. He scooted around Mr. Ward and fled up the steps two at a time.

"Come on, Kev!"

"I'm going home, Bantam!" Kev shouted after him. "See you tomorrow!"

Bantam gave a quick, final look at Mr. Ward and practically shriveled under the man's burning eyes. Some people, he thought, just had no tolerance for anything. Not even a harmless old frog.

7

IN his room Bantam took the glove and ballpoint pen out of his pocket and looked at them again. There was something about the pen he had seen before, but had not thought anything about: The words on the pen were pretty much worn off, indicating that whoever owned it had been here at Fugitive House a long time.

The next morning Kev came over with a plan. "Let's see if we can get into the cave from the lake side," he said. "We might be able to climb up to it from shore."

"Okay," said Bantam.

They walked along the edge of the cliff to the steps opposite Old Farley's shack, and descended them to the beach. It was the shortest way to the cave. A small boat was on shore.

"Whose boat?" asked Bantam.

"Old Farley's. I'm surprised he's not on the lake now—fishing. He'll probably fish tonight."

"Tonight?"

"He fishes at night a lot," said Kev.

They started toward the cave, but could not get within forty feet of it. There was no shoreline to walk on. They tried to scale the rock wall, but it was too steep.

Then Bantam saw something that brought a glimmer of hope. "Kev, look! A rope ladder!"

It was looped around the stump of a tree and hung down the cliff to the cave entrance.

"Whose is it?" queried Bantam. "Ever seen it before?"

"No. It could've been there for years, for all I know."

"Shall we climb down it?"

"Why not?"

They went back up to the edge of the cliff. Bantam descended the rope ladder first, noticing that there was something unusual about it. It had rained a lot yesterday, but still the rope seemed dry. Certainly the morning sun had not been out long enough to have dried it if it had been wet.

He paused, wondering whether to keep

going down or to retreat.

"What're you stopping for?" asked Kev.

"This rope looks as if it's just been put here," said Bantam.

"Think someone's down there?"

"I don't know."

"Well, what shall we do?"

Bantam thought a minute. "Let's keep going."

They descended to the cave. The shoulders of rock on either side of the narrow stream of water were wide, the ceiling high enough to walk under without stooping. Bantam felt his spine tingle as he gazed far into the black depths of the cave.

"Don't see anyone," he said.

"Let's go in farther," said Kev bravely.

They started to move slowly. "We should have brought a flashlight," said Bantam.

The deeper into the cave they went, the cooler it became. Should have brought sweaters, too, thought Bantam.

Suddenly a light, dim at first and growing brighter by the second, shone ahead of them. It could have been a hundred feet away, or a hundred yards. The tunnel made distance hard to judge. The boys stopped, Kev so close to Bantam that Bantam could feel his warm breath against his ear.

"Let's get out of here!" Kev whispered.

"Wait!"

Seconds later a man appeared from around a bend, his shadow bobbing on the walls around him. He was advancing at a hasty pace—as hasty, that is, as his short steps allowed him. In that moment the boys recognized him. Old Farley!

"You!" Old Farley hissed. "Get out of here! *Get out of here!*"

They turned and ran. Up the ladder they

scurried, Bantam's feet kicking Kev on the head several times before the boys reached the top. They hurried and hid behind a boulder that stood perched near the edge of the cliff.

With pounding hearts, they waited.

8

OLD Farley climbed up from the edge of the cliff. He looked around, then picked up the rope ladder, folded it into a pile and walked off with it to his shack. He didn't have the light now. He must have left it in the cave.

"Since he's got a ladder, he's probably gone down there a lot of times," surmised Bantam. "Wonder what there is down there that he might want so much."

They watched Old Farley shuffle to his shack and disappear inside.

"Let's talk with him," suggested Bantam.

"Talk with him? Are you crazy? He won't talk with anybody."

"How do you know?"

"*Everybody* knows it."

"Did *you* ever try?"

"No. Why should I, if he doesn't want to talk?"

Bantam stood up. "Come on. He can't do any more than shoo us away."

Kev, rising, shook his head. "Boy, for a peewee you've got more guts than brains."

They walked for a while along the brink of the cliff, then cut inland toward Old Farley's shack. Far out on the lake a sailboat was cruising along quietly and speedily, its tall white sails billowing like pillows.

Cautiously the boys approached the side of the shack, their footsteps muffled by the grass. As they passed the window, they could see the old man pouring water from a kettle into a coffeepot. He carried the pot across the small room to a four-burner stove, set it on a burner and turned it on. Instantly a circle of blue flame leaped up under it. Then he went to a small refrigerator, took out a paper bag and carried it to the table. It must be the bag of food Tony Torro had left for the old man a couple of nights ago.

Old Farley set the bag down, took out a cellophane-wrapped package and unwrapped it. It was filled with chicken legs and breasts.

"Does that look good!" whispered Bantam. "Come on!"

They walked to the door. Bantam knocked. A moment later Old Farley stood before them, staring through wide, pale eyes. "Seen you two down in the cave," he said. "What were you doing in there? What do you want?"

"We—we just wanted to know if you had seen anything down there, Old—I mean, Mr. Farley," stammered Bantam.

"That's none of your goldarn business! Now get out of here! Get!"

The boys turned and beat it up the road as if a swarm of bees were after them. They slowed down to a walk, glanced back over their shoulders and saw that Old Farley had gone back into his shack.

"What's the matter with him?" said Bantam, baffled.

"He's gone cuckoo," said Kev.

"He's a lot different this time than the other time I saw him," observed Bantam.

"He's sure mad about something."

"Not only mad. Scared, too. Maybe of something he saw in the cave." But what could be in the cave that would scare Old Farley? He must be familiar with the place. He probably knew every nook and cranny in there.

They climbed the steps to the porch of the inn and walked down to the far end. Bantam sat on the wooden railing with his back against the building. Kev sat facing him with his back against the corner post.

"If Mr. Ward would give us the key for the door leading to the cave, we could maybe find out what had scared Old Farley," said Bantam.

"And find the painting," added Kev.

"Did you tell Michelle about the painting?" Bantam asked.

"Heck, no. She'd go out of her mind thinking that the guy she was nuts about was a thief."

A blue station wagon drove up the road, pulled onto the driveway in front of the steps and stopped. A man and a woman were sitting in front, another couple in the seat behind them. The driver got out and climbed the steps to the front door. He shot a glance at the boys, then went into the building.

A little while later he was out again. "All right," he said to the three people in the car, "let's unload."

Bantam watched them haul out suitcases from the back end of the station wagon, but his mind was on a remark he had made to Kev. Get the key from Mr. Ward? If Mr. Ward was the only person who had a key to the door that led to the cave, then who else could have entered it? Nobody!

"Kev! Mr. Ward is the only person with a key! If anyone carried a painting into the cave, who else could it be but him?"

"That's crazy. He wouldn't steal a painting. Not Mr. Ward. He's well off. Why would he steal a painting?"

"This one's worth over a hundred thousand dollars!" whispered Bantam tensely. "That's a lot of money!"

"But he wouldn't steal a painting!" insisted Kev. "Do you think he'd sneak down to Terry's house, take his car, steal the painting, hide it in the cave, then drive Terry's car back? Not Mr. Ward. He's a peculiar character, but he wouldn't do a crazy thing like that. Not him."

"But he's the only person with a key! Your grandfather Polkie said so!" Crazy as it might seem to Kev, and to him, too, Bantam could see no other explanation. He had seen the person take a large, square-shaped object into the basement. He and Kev had searched for it and couldn't find it. Therefore it must have been taken into the cave. And if Mr. Ward was the only person who had a key to get into the cave, who but Mr. Ward *could* have taken the painting in there? And that ballpoint pen. And that glove. Those could be his, too.

The day grew hotter. By mid-afternoon the sun was like a ladle pouring heat down on the land. Bantam, trying to forget about the painting and the cave for a while, walked to Kev's place for a swim.

"Why don't you have your aunt and uncle come, too?" Mr. Wilson suggested. "There's no place like the beach today."

"Thanks," said Bantam, pleased at the suggestion. "Can I call them on your phone?"

"Of course."

It turned out that not only Aunt Janet and Uncle Dick came, but so did a person Bantam and Kev least expected. Mr. Ward! His wife, a tall gray-haired woman, came with him.

They all went swimming. Well, not exactly. Mr. and Mrs. Ward just seemed to be sitting in the water. It wasn't until the children—Kev, Bantam and Nancy—kept urging Mr. Ward to take a ride on the water skis that you might say Mr. Ward had really gone swimming.

Announcing to everyone that he used to be a champ water-skier in his day, he accepted the children's challenge. He was doing all right while the water skis were still underwater. The moment the motorboat, driven by Mr. Wilson, pulled him out of the water, Mr. Ward had trouble. He lost his balance and toppled over. It was then that he had to swim until Mr. Wilson steered the boat up alongside of him and dragged him aboard.

"Lost my touch," puffed Mr. Ward. "And, I guess, my youth."

The children laughed. And Bantam thought: If Mr. Ward was the person who had taken Terry's car and then had stolen the painting, he was indeed a great actor. No. Mr. Ward just couldn't be a thief. He was convinced of it now.

After supper Bantam went to his room for his telescope to look at the boats sailing on the lake. It wasn't on the shelf where he had left it. Puzzled, he looked in the closet, under the bed and everywhere he could think of.

No telescope.

9

"AUNT JANET, have you seen my telescope?"

"Isn't it in your room?"

"No." Bantam turned questioning eyes at Uncle Dick.

"I haven't, either," replied Uncle Dick. "Did you look your room over thoroughly?"

"I practically turned it upside down," replied Bantam. "It's not in there."

"That's funny." Uncle Dick went out of the kitchen and Bantam followed him. This time Uncle Dick practically turned Bantam's room upside down, too. He couldn't find the telescope, either. Then they looked through the living room, while Aunt Janet looked through the kitchen.

"You didn't let Kev take it, did you?" asked Uncle Dick.

"I know I didn't," said Bantam worriedly.

Uncle Dick went into the kitchen and picked up the telephone.

"Who are you going to call, Uncle Dick?"

"Mr. Ward. I'll tell him your telescope's missing, just in case someone finds it."

"Oh, don't do that, Uncle Dick," pleaded Bantam. Fear gripped him as he foresaw what calling up Mr. Ward would mean. "Please don't call him."

"Why not?"

Bantam's face grew hot. He hadn't wanted to say anything about Mr. Ward to Uncle Dick. He'd have to tell him the whole story—about the stolen painting, the ballpoint pen, the glove and the locked door in the basement, the door for which only Mr. Ward had a key.

"He won't know anything about it, Uncle

Dick. Even if someone found it, he wouldn't tell Mr. Ward, would he?"

Uncle Dick looked at his nephew with growing suspicion in his eyes. "Something bothering you, Bantam? Something else beside your missing telescope?"

Bantam looked away. The moment was coming. Now that Uncle Dick suspected something, he wouldn't stop asking questions until he had all the answers.

"Better tell me about it, Bantam," persuaded Uncle Dick. "Are you in trouble with Mr. Ward? Or with someone else? Speak up, Bantam."

The tone of Uncle Dick's voice started off softly, then became sharp and hurting. Bantam's heart sank. Just when he was beginning to think that Aunt Janet and Uncle Dick trusted him, he had become mixed up in a plot that was both mysterious and dangerous. He had done nothing wrong. He had simply seen a car below his window that turned out to be Terry Lott's. That small incident had started the whole thing.

"Come on, Bantam," Uncle Dick's voice prodded him again. "What trouble are you in now?"

He didn't like the sound of those words. Uncle Dick was already passing sentence on him.

"I'm in no trouble. It's about the car I saw that night below my window. I told you and Aunt Janet about it."

"I remember," said Uncle Dick. "What about it?" His voice sounded softer again.

Bantam told him. He told him about seeing a person—he wasn't sure if it was Terry because it was too dark to see—carrying a large, square-shaped object into the basement. And that the object was probably the famous Von Rogen painting stolen from the Baker Art Museum in Brice. He told about how he and Kev had gone into the basement to search for the painting, but had not found it. And about the ballpoint pen, the glove and the padlocked door.

"And the only person who has a key to that door is Mr. Ward," finished Bantam.

"Kev's grandfather Polkie said so. He seemed sure. He seemed to know a lot about Mr. Ward and Fugitive House."

"So that's it," said Uncle Dick. "You think it might be Mr. Ward who had stolen the painting and hidden it in the cave, since he's the only one who has a key?"

Bantam shrugged. "It seems so. I don't know."

"Let's see the pen and the glove," asked Uncle Dick.

Bantam showed them to him. "Hmm," murmured Uncle Dick. "Someone might have used gloves to keep from leaving fingerprints. And this pen. It's like the one Mr. Ward gave us, but it's plenty worn."

The phone rang. Uncle Dick picked it up. "Yes?" He listened for a while, then smiled. "Okay, Mr. Ward. Thanks very much. We'll be out there. By the way, Mr. Ward, my nephew Bantam can't seem to locate his telescope. I'd appreciate very much your letting me know if someone reports finding it. Okay. Thanks, Mr. Ward. Goodbye."

Bantam sat staring at his uncle. Uncle Dick winked at him. "No one's reported it yet. Don't worry. It'll turn up sometime."

Aunt Janet came in and asked, "What did Mr. Ward want?"

"A group of people are going to put on an acrobatic and juggling act on the lawn at eight o'clock," answered Uncle Dick. "Guess they'd like to have an audience."

"Fine!" Aunt Janet glanced at the wall clock. "Seven-thirty. I'd better freshen up a bit and put on another dress."

The group of acrobats turned out to be the same foursome Bantam had seen drive up to the hotel during the day. They used no equipment other than a long, wide mat which had been placed on the lawn. Kev was there, too. And Nancy and Michelle, their parents, Grandpa Polkie and some of the other neighbors. Everyone except Old Farley. But Bantam had not expected to see him there, anyway.

One of the acrobats introduced the group as the Four Eldoras. They started their act by cartwheeling around the mat, then somersaulting without the use of their hands. And they performed many other acrobatic and tumbling stunts.

But none of it was new to Bantam, or to Kev. They had seen the same act dozens of times on television.

Bantam nudged Kev on the elbow. "Let's take a walk," he said softly.

"Where to?"

"Into the hotel."

Bantam looked toward Aunt Janet and Uncle Dick. Both were sitting on lawn chairs, apparently engrossed in the act.

"What's on your mind?" Kev asked once they were inside Fugitive House.

"I was thinking of the trapdoor Grandpa Polkie had said was under a rug in the pantry," said Bantam. He looked around. The place seemed empty. Apparently everyone was outside watching the Four Eldoras.

"Do the police still suspect Terry?"

"Yes. And he still says he knows nothing about the painting."

"Come on," said Bantam. "Let's find that trapdoor."

They went into the kitchen and crossed over to the pantry, a small room on the rear side of the building. The smell of fresh bread, onions and vinegar filled the room.

The boys looked at the floor. "It's covered *all over* with a rug," whispered Bantam, his hopes vanishing for a moment.

The rug was a piece of linoleum, covered with black scuff marks and dirt. Otherwise it seemed hardly worn.

Bantam went to one side of the room and started to reach for the edge of the rug to lift it. Just then he heard the outside door open and close, and the sound of cautious footsteps in the hall.

10

BANTAM rose quickly and tiptoed behind the door, motioning Kev to follow him. Standing like statues they listened to the footsteps approach, then fade as the person apparently walked into another room. Seconds later the footsteps sounded again in the hall.

"Kev! Bantam!" Nancy's voice!

"What in heck does she want?" whispered Kev disgustedly.

Nancy's footsteps came closer, then seemed to pause on the threshold of the kitchen doorway. "Kev! Bantam! Are you in here? Please answer if you are!"

Kev looked at Bantam. "What shall we do?"

"We might as well tell her we're here," said Bantam. "Then tell her to scram."

They walked out from behind the door and into the kitchen. Nancy's eyes sprang wide as doorknobs.

"What do you want?" hissed Kev.

"What are you two doing in here?" Nancy asked with bewilderment.

"Looking for my telescope," Bantam answered, hating to lie to her. Later he'd tell her the truth. "It turned up missing."

"Did Mom and Dad send you?" asked Kev.

"Yes. And Bantam's aunt and uncle know I'm here, too." She looked at Bantam. "What telescope?"

"*My* telescope." Bantam was beginning to be exasperated.

"Nancy, please, please scram out of here, will you?" pleaded her brother. "Before Mom and Dad come looking for you."

Nancy wrinkled her nose at him and turned her attention back to Bantam. "May

I help? Three searchers are better than two."

"No," said Kev emphatically, before Bantam could answer.

"We can search for it ourselves, Nancy," said Bantam, in as pleasant a voice as he could muster. He didn't want Nancy to get angry with him.

"Okay," she snapped, and spun on her heel so fast her dress swirled. Seconds later the boys heard the door slamming shut behind her. They exchanged a satisfied look, then returned to the pantry. Bantam began lifting the edge of the rug. It crackled as it tore loose from the floor. Kev helped him roll it up until nearly a third of it was off.

Still no trapdoor.

"Hope Grandpa knows what he's talking about," said Kev.

"So do I," confessed Bantam.

They pulled the rug back a few more inches . . . then a few more inches. Maybe we should have started from the other end, thought Bantam.

And then they saw a crack going across the floor boards. About two feet from it, running parallel with it, was another. Hopes rising, the boys pulled the rug farther back and saw that the cracks were about two feet long, indicating a trapdoor about two feet square. There was no ring—nothing—to lift it with.

"How do we open it?" asked Kev.

Bantam got a knife from the kitchen, poked it into a crack, then pried. The board lifted with a soft *whoosh!* He got a firm grip on it with his other hand, and with Kev's help lifted the board clear. A cold, dank draft shot up against their faces. A ladder led down into a grim-looking sea of blackness.

Bantam was gripped with excitement. "Hold this, Kev. I'll run upstairs and get our flashlight."

He was back in a minute. He switched on the flashlight, shone it into the darkness below and stared down into a round tunnel some twenty feet deep. He started to descend the ladder. Kev followed.

They reached the bottom and Bantam flashed the light around the bleak stone walls, a stream of water flowing in a crack on the cave floor, and toward a wide room far ahead that seemed to have furniture in it. He shone the light in the opposite direction and saw that the cave seemed to have its beginning less than twenty feet away, perhaps somewhere under the road that faced Fugitive House. Here it narrowed to a small, eye-shaped opening.

He turned the light on the furnished room again and started for it, Kev close beside him. What if someone entered the pantry now? thought Bantam. What if the Four Eldoras had finished their act and Tony Torro or Mel Sweeney, or even Mr. Ward, stepped into the pantry for something? They'd see the rug rolled back and the trapdoor open and . . .

"Let's turn back, Bantam," Kev whispered. "I don't like this."

"Turn back? Now?"

"I'm scared."

"So am I. But we're here. And there's

some furniture. Look. A table and chairs, and a cupboard. They must have been used by slaves over a hundred years ago."

When they reached the room the boys' awe became three-fold. Besides the table and a score of chairs, there were wooden cups, dishes and bowls in an open cupboard. Bantam began to imagine frightened slaves sitting and eating around the large table, and his skin crawled.

"Let's get out of here, Bantam," Kev said, as if he were imagining the same things, too. "This place gives me the chills."

"But the painting. It must be here some place," insisted Bantam.

He cast the light over the shelves. He gasped with joy. Beside the cups and bowls was a box. A very familiar cardboard box.

"Kev!" cried Bantam. "It's my telescope!"

He picked it up and by its weight he knew that the telescope was in it.

"Now let's go," said Kev anxiously.

"Just a second more," said Bantam. "Let's look at the bed."

A rusty iron bed was beyond the dining room with old, sagging springs on it. There was no mattress. Bantam's flashlight beam caught something behind it, and his heart practically stopped.

A large, square-shaped object covered with black plastic!

"Kev! Hold this light!"

He pulled the object out from behind the bed and tore off the plastic. Kev shone the light on it. It was a painting! A painting of some people working in a field! And in the lower righthand corner was a name: *Von Rogen.*

Was that all there was to it? he thought. Was *this* supposed to be worth over a hundred thousand dollars?

There was a sound behind them. The boys froze. Slowly they turned around. In the tar-black darkness beyond the reach of Bantam's flashlight they could see nothing.

"Let's run!" said Kev.

11

BANTAM covered the painting, placed it behind the bed and started running toward the opposite direction from which they had heard the noise—away from the trapdoor. His only thought was that the person who had stolen the painting had entered the cave after them.

"Hey! Come back here!" a voice boomed. The sound of it ricocheted against the walls and became jumbled and muffled.

Bantam accidentally kicked a small stone and sent it bouncing ahead of them. Where's the end of this cave? he wondered, looking ahead for a sign of daylight. How far do we have to run?

And then a thought struck him like a hard blow. "Kev! What'll we do when we get to the mouth of the cave? We can't get out. We're stuck in here."

"Then we're licked!" Kev groaned.

The cave curved sharply to their right, and ahead of them was a huge round eye of light. But what help was it? They couldn't climb out; the cliff was too steep. Maybe they could jump.

They reached the edge of the cave and looked down. The narrow, silken waterfall plummeted down into the lake some ten feet below in a soft, musical hum.

"Let's jump, Kev," said Bantam. He was about to throw the box with the telescope in it into the lake when a voice shouted, "Hey, boys! Wait! It's me—Tony!"

They spun. Tony Torro was running toward them, his bearlike body wobbling visibly. He was waving desperately, his thick curls bouncing on his head.

The boys stared at each other. "Let's jump!" yelled Kev, panic-stricken. "Come on!"

Bantam grabbed his arm. "No! It wasn't him I saw. I know it wasn't. Tony's much bigger than the person I saw carrying the painting from the car."

The boys looked at Tony Torro, who had stopped running and was walking toward them, breathing hard.

"You kids run me ragged," he gasped. "I ain't young any more. Now what's the big idea opening up the trapdoor and sneaking down here like a coupla thieves? If it was anybody but me that had seen you it could be your hides."

"We thought you were the guy who had stolen the painting and you were trying to stop us," said Bantam honestly.

Tony's dark eyes rounded. "What painting?"

"The Von Rogen painting that was stolen from the art museum in Brice. It's worth a hundred thousand dollars. Haven't you heard about it?"

Tony looked from one boy to the other, frowning with bewilderment. "Sure, I heard about it. But what's it got to do with you two little monkeys sneaking down here? You expect to find it in this cave?"

For a moment the boys hesitated to speak.

"Well, answer me!" exploded Tony. "What makes you think the painting's in this cave?"

"We've found it," said Bantam.

"You what?"

"We found the painting," Kev joined in. "It's behind the bed."

The curls on Tony's head seemed to quiver. "How in saints name did you boys know that the painting was in here?"

They explained the whole story to him. "The police think Terry did it," Bantam added. "They think he had stolen it because his car was parked near the art museum that night. And it was, because it was the same car I saw drive up behind Fugitive House. A second later I saw somebody get out of it with the painting and carry it into the basement."

Tony's brows shot skyward. "You *saw* the painting?"

Bantam nodded. "Only I didn't know it was the painting then. It was pretty dark. But it was the painting all right."

"You figured it was the stolen painting *after* you heard the report over the radio and *after* Terry was picked up by the police? Is that it?"

"Yes."

"Okay. Let's pick up the painting and call the police. Let me have your flashlight, Banty."

Bantam handed it to him, convinced that it wasn't Tony who had stolen the painting. But who was it? Sweeney? Mr. Ward? *Or was it really Terry?*

Tony started back into the inner depths of the cave, the boys trailing close behind him. They approached the old iron bed. Tony picked up the painting, pulled off the plastic cover and focused the light on it.

"Hey, it's really a beautiful picture!" he said. "But whoever would give a hundred thousand dollars for it has money to throw away. I wonder what the guy who stole it figured to do with it? Why did he bring it here? Why didn't he take it home? Well, come on. Let's get out of here before old man Ward starts snooping around and finds the trapdoor open."

They walked toward the ladder and Bantam thought, almost with disappointment, It's over with now. We've found the paint

ing. Will the police ever find out who stole it and hid it here in the cave? Was it really Terry Lott? Or was it someone who used his car to let the blame fall on Terry? Bantam couldn't guess what the criminal's intention was, but he hated to think that he might go unpunished.

They arrived at the ladder that led to the trapdoor. Tony cast the beam of the flashlight up, and Bantam froze.

"It's closed!" he cried.

At that instant a chuckle rippled in the darkness to their left. A strong beam of light pinned them against the ladder.

"Drop the flashlight, Tony," said a low voice. "Drop it, or I'll shoot."

12

TONY switched off the flashlight, lowered it to within a foot of the floor, then dropped it.

"Now move," ordered the voice. "Toward the furniture."

That voice! Bantam recognized it now. "Sweeney!" Tony roared. "You! What is this—a gag?"

Mel Sweeney's voice answered with a sinister warning. "Don't do as I say and you'll find out whether it's a gag or not. Move. Toward the furniture."

His bright flashlight pushed the darkness aside, and the boys and Tony headed for the large furnished room. There they turned and faced Sweeney, though they were unable to see his face above the glaring light.

"You're making a big mistake, Sweeney," warned Tony.

"Skip the lecture, Tony," grunted Sweeney. "I've had enough of them. Sit down."

Tony and the boys sat. The light swung to the wall and to the upright side of a cupboard where a coiled rope hung on a long nail. Sweeney lifted the rope off the nail and tossed it at Bantam's feet.

"There's enough there for the three of you," he said. "Tie up El Torro first, Bantam. Hands behind the chair, Mr. Torro."

Tony obeyed and Bantam tied up his hands, trying not to make the rope too tight and hoping Sweeney would not notice. But Sweeney did.

"Pull that rope tight, kid," he snapped angrily, kicking Bantam on the seat of his pants.

Afraid now, Bantam pulled the rope

tighter, wrapping it around and around Tony's wrists and then tying a couple of knots in it.

"Okay. Now get one of those knives hanging in the cupboard and cut the rope. Then tie up your friend."

Bantam followed the order, still trying hard to believe that it was really Melvin Sweeney pointing the gun at them and snapping orders.

"Okay," said Sweeney. "Now sit down and I'll tie you up."

He placed the light on the table so that it shone on Tony and the boys, and set his gun beside it. Then he proceeded to tie Bantam's hands behind the chair.

"Ouch," said Bantam.

"Hurt? Good. This should teach you not to pry into other people's business."

"Even if it's rotten business?" broke in Tony.

Sweeney laughed. "Maybe so, El Torro. But after this is over I'll be sitting pretty. I'll be able to settle down and live a nice, happy life. There," he said. Bantam felt him tie the last knot that bound his hands securely. "That should do it."

"You must be the person I saw carry the painting into the basement," said Bantam. "And who lost the glove and ballpoint pen."

"And the one who took Terry's car," added Kev.

"Right on all counts," said Sweeney. "I was careless about the glove and pen. Hurried too much."

"Why did you pick Terry's car?" asked Kev bluntly. "Why not somebody else's?"

"Well, Terry and I bowled and water-skied a few times together. I know the police suspect him, but they won't arrest him. How can they if they can't prove he stole the painting?"

"How were you able to take his car?" Kev asked. "He never leaves the key in it. I'm sure of that."

"Brains, kid. A couple of weeks ago I told him I couldn't get my car running, and he let me borrow his. Then I had a duplicate key made. I did the same thing with old man Ward's key for the door leading into the cave from the basement. Of course I had to steal it from him. That key is sacred to the old skinflint."

"I suppose you saw the trapdoor open, got suspicious and closed it, then came down here through the basement," said Tony.

Sweeney chuckled. "Right."

"You're making a foolish mistake, Sweeney. You'd better change your mind about the painting and take it back. You do that the cops might be easy on you."

Sweeney laughed. "Change my mind now? Tonight? The very night an agent's coming to take the painting off my hands for fifty thousand dollars? No, El Torro. I'm going through with it. You and the boys are going to sit here till it's all over."

"And how long is that supposed to be?"

"Till midnight."

"Midnight?"

"That's right. Midnight. That's the hour he's coming to take the painting. And I'm going with him."

13

WHO'S coming for the painting?" asked Tony.

Sweeney's laughter was a rumble of extreme pleasure in the darkness. "I'm not mentioning any names, El Torro, except that he's an agent for a big art collector. You and the kids might sit here a long time. Long enough to die, maybe, unless somebody finds you first. And if you did not die, and I told you the name of the man I'm selling the painting to, he'd be in an embarrassing position. Wouldn't he?"

"So would you," said Bantam.

The light swung and glared like a blazing

eye at him. "Not really. I won't be around to worry about it."

"How did you know about this guy who wants the Von Rogen painting?" inquired Tony.

Sweeney chuckled. "Full of questions, aren't you, El Torro? Well, I met his agent at a bar in Brice a few weeks ago. We got to talking. After he told me he works for a rich, eccentric art collector, he admitted a few other important things. This rich art collector lives on an island and has a terrific obsession for famous old paintings. If he wants a painting bad enough, he'll make an offer. If the owner won't sell, this art collector leaves it up to his agent. So far, he has always gotten every painting he was after. A cunning man, I'd say. Wouldn't you, El Torro?"

"And you're playing along with the agent," said Tony. "You want to land back in jail again, don't you? The next time it will be twenty years, Sweeney. Not six months."

The light swung to Tony's face. "How did

you know about that?" Sweeney's voice lashed like a whip.

"I've known it a long time, Sweeney," said Tony. "Mr. Ward told me. The first time it was theft, too, wasn't it? A gas station. Now you're gambling your next twenty years—"

"Shut up, Torro," said Sweeney. "Shut up or I'll blast this light over your head."

Shivers slithered up and down Bantam's back. All at once Sweeney seemed like a much different person than he was upstairs in the kitchen, or even a few minutes ago. His voice was sinister and threatening.

"They'll get you, Sweeney," reminded Tony. "They'll get you somehow, and your goose will be cooked forever."

"Shut up, I said! I think I better put a gag over your big mouth. You talk too much, El Torro."

Sweeney set the flashlight on the table, pulled off Tony's apron, ripped off a piece and tied it over Tony's mouth.

"That'll shut you up," he said. "Maybe I'd better put gags over your mouths, too," he said to the boys. "Yes, I think I'd better. And you'd better not scream, you understand? Scream and I'll knock you cold."

He ripped a couple of more pieces from the apron and tied them around the boys' mouths. "There," he said, and laughed. "Now you can scream your heads off."

He picked up the light. "Where was I? Oh, yes. The agent. He told me he had offered a hundred thousand dollars for *The Workers*, but the museum refused to sell. So I made a suggestion. Would he give me fifty thousand if I got it for him? You know the answer. I found out that the caretaker lives on the third floor of the museum. Which was fine. The toughest part was prying off the iron bars of the cellar windows in the rear of the building. Once I was inside, the rest was easy. Tonight at midnight I deliver the painting and get my money."

"Ha?" said Tony around the gag in his mouth.

"How?"

Tony nodded.

"The agent's coming over by boat. That's why I took your telescope, Bantam," Sweeney said. "I couldn't trust you after you'd gotten suspicious about the painting. I didn't want to take a chance of your stargazing again tonight and then spotting a boat coming here to the cave. You'd shout your head off to your aunt and ruin it all."

He looked at his wristwatch. "Well, it's a few minutes after nine. I'd better get back upstairs. See you at midnight. Don't run away, will you?" He slouched off into the ink-black depths of the cave, the flashlight cutting a cone-shaped path ahead of him.

Tony and the boys heard the basement door open and close. Sweeney was gone. Gone, at least, until midnight when he would deliver the painting for fifty thousand dollars and leave with it on the boat. Where was he going then? Out of the country? Probably, thought Bantam hopelessly.

A chair squeaked, and Bantam guessed it

was Tony trying to break loose from his bonds. It was Tony, for he began to grunt. A few moments later the sounds stopped, and Bantam heard Tony breathing as though he were tired.

Then Bantam heard Kev trying to break loose from his bonds, heard the chair scrape over the rock floor and then heard it topple over. "Oo!" Kev cried.

Bantam heard Kev breathing close to the floor. Kev, it seemed, wasn't able to get his chair back up on its legs.

Bantam tried to stand on his feet, but his hands' being tied behind the chair made it impossible. He tried to lift his arms over the back of the chair. He couldn't do that, either. Fear gripped him, and cold, clammy sweat drenched his face and the palms of his hands.

He heard Kev struggling again to straighten up his chair. Finally he heard the chair's legs plop on the floor, and knew that Kev had succeeded.

If only someone would think about looking for them in the cave. But who would? No one. Not even Mr. Ward would think about it, for wasn't he supposed to have the only key for the door to it? And it looked like nobody except Tony and the boys had used the trapdoor for years.

Only Old Farley could possibly find them here. But something—or someone—had scared him away, too. Scared him so that he might never re-enter the cave. Was it Sweeney? Was it he who had frightened Old Farley in the cave? If so, he probably warned him not to go in it again.

Bantam shut his eyes and shook his head in hopeless despair. Sweeney was the last person he would dream would ever do a thing like this. And if Tony and Kev and he couldn't get out of their bonds, Sweeney might get away and live happily ever after, just as he said he would—unless the police caught him first. By then it might be too late for the three in the cave.

While he sat Bantam could hear Tony Torro's heavy breathing almost drowning out Kev's much quieter breathing. They seemed to have given up trying to get loose.

Bantam had no idea how long they had been tied when his steadily working mind came up with an idea. He had seen some wooden cups and bowls on a shelf. If he were able to get them . . .

He tipped the chair over carefully upon its side, falling with it and striking the floor gently with his shoulder. He remembered that the shelf was on the other side of the table, so he pulled himself to his knees and began crawling around the table toward it.

He circled the table, struggled to his feet and just made it. Carefully he lowered his head, felt his chin touch the shelf, then moved it in search of a wooden cup or a bowl. His cheek brushed against a cup and toppled it over. His heart thumped with hope. Opening his mouth wide he gripped the edge of the cup between his lower jaw and the gag, carried it to the stream of water, and dropped it. He heard it splash.

Then he returned to the shelf and found a

bowl. This he gripped in his mouth the same way he had gripped the cup, carried it to the stream and dropped it. The bowl missed the stream, clattered on the floor and laid still.

Discouragement overtook him. He soon found the bowl, kicked it gently and heard it fall into the stream. Then he heard it banging against the rock sides as the stream carried it away. All at once he realized that it was night and almost impossible for the cup and bowl to be seen on the lake. Even if someone did spot them, how would he know where they came from? Bantam's hope sank to rock bottom.

He felt a sneeze coming. Ah-choo! On top of everything he was catching a cold.

14

TIME seemed to stand still. Now and then the silence was broken by either Kev's or Tony's chair as it squeaked in its old wooden joints. They were trying again to break loose from the ropes, but were having no success.

Bantam tried hard to free his wrists, too. The harder he tried the tighter the rope seemed to become, and the sorer his wrists. Ah-choo! His sneezes were coming more often, too.

He tried to stand on his feet again, but couldn't. He toppled the chair to its side as he had done before, then rose to his knees and then to his feet. A triumphant smile tugged at his mouth. He was little, but not helpless. Maybe someday he could prove that to Aunt Janet and Uncle Dick.

But if he didn't get out of here alive, how would he be able to prove that?

He listened for the sound of the water and started to walk alongside of it. Left foot. Right foot. Left foot. Right. Then his left foot slid. He lost his balance. Chair and he fell into the stream.

The water was icy cold and he gasped for breath. He struggled out, and lay panting on the hard floor beside the stream. Tears stung his eyes. He shut them tight and bit down hard on the cloth. This was no time to cry.

He shivered and sneezed again. "You'd better come in where it's warm or you'll catch your death of cold," Mom used to say. Well, he would certainly like to do that now. But he couldn't. He was too cold from the water, too tired to hardly move. He just wanted to lie there.

After awhile he rose to his feet again. The chair seemed heavier than ever. He plopped on its seat, closed his eyes and laid back his head. He fell asleep and dreamed he was naked and cold and running in some dark place. He awoke, shivering and scared.

A light flickered in the darkness, grew brighter and brighter. Soon shadows danced on the walls. Footsteps approached, and someone came around the bend from the direction of the cave's mouth. Presently he was standing there in the darkness with the light shining full on them. Standing and not saying a word.

"Ahg! Ahg!" Bantam muttered, and wriggled in his chair to show that he wanted to be set free. Kev and Tony Torro frantically copied his actions. Surely the person must know what they were trying to say.

"He tied you here, didn't he?" came Old Farley's voice suddenly. "He's mean, that Sweeney is. Very mean."

He approached Bantam first and removed the gag from his mouth. Bantam took a deep, welcome breath. "Thank you, Old Farley! I mean, Mr. Farley. Now, please, untie the rope."

Old Farley fumbled with the rope with

one hand while holding the flashlight with his other. "I was fishing," he said, "and saw the moon shining on a couple of things in the water. I got curious and rowed over to 'em and picked 'em up, and recognized them as a cup and a bowl from this cave. I come here a lot, you know. It's so much cooler than it is in my little house."

Bantam smiled happily.

"Early this morning I heard the folks around Fugitive House searching for you boys and Mr. Torro," continued Old Farley. "When I saw the cup and bowl I figured maybe you three were trapped here by Sweeney and had thrown them in to get help. Guess I figured right. Sweeney's a mean one, he is. I met him in here yesterday. He chased me out. Warned me never to come in here again or he'd kill me. So I knew he was up to no good."

A new sound came from behind them. A light sprang against the walls from the direction of the basement door.

"It's Sweeney!" whispered Bantam. "Hurry, hurry!"

An instant later the rope loosened from Bantam's wrists, and he wriggled his hands free. Then he leaped off the chair and took the flashlight from Old Farley.

"Let's run, Mr. Farley! We'll get help for the others."

He raced ahead to the bend, then cut to the right toward the mouth of the cave.

"Wait! Wait!" Old Farley's plea came from behind Bantam.

Bantam swung the light around and saw the old man trailing far behind, hurrying as fast as he could, which wasn't fast at all. "Come on, Mr. Farley! Come on!"

But all the pleading in the world couldn't speed up Old Farley.

I ought to go on alone, Bantam thought. *I can get out of here much faster by myself.* He started to run. But after running twenty feet or so he stopped. No. He couldn't leave Old Farley. Not alone in total darkness. Old Farley might stumble into the water and hurt himself. He might get deathly scared of being left there at the mercy of Melvin Sweeney.

Bantam cast the light in front of Old Farley's feet and waited for the old man to catch up. He looked back over his shoulder and saw the mouth of the cave in the distance, a dark patch of blue surrounded by pitch blackness. It seemed a million miles away.

At last Old Farley was near. Bantam turned and hurried on. "Come on, Mr. Farley. Come on."

A light sprang up behind them and against the walls. There was a sound of running feet. Bantam peered over his shoulder and panic hit him as he saw the bright, glaring eye of a strong flashlight come into view.

"Bantam!" Sweeney's voice cracked like a whip. "Stop or I'll shoot! You, too, Farley!"

For a couple of seconds Bantam pondered on what to do. *If we both stop,* he thought, *Sweeney will tie us up and succeed with his plan. I've got to keep running. I've got to get out of this cave.*

He turned off the flashlight and started

running as hard as he could toward the cave's mouth. Far behind him came Sweeney's angry shout: "Bantam, come back here! *Come back here!*"

Bantam waited for the sound of a shot. It didn't come. He reached the mouth of the cave and leaped over the narrow stream of water to the side where he expected Old Farley's rope ladder to be. And stopped dead.

There, below him and to his left, was a motorboat being drawn up onto the narrow shore. The men were here for Sweeney and the painting.

Panting breathlessly, Bantam looked for the rope ladder, found it, and started to climb it. He hadn't taken more than four steps up when he felt a tug on the ladder and heard Sweeney's voice.

"Bantam! Don't go any farther."

15

SWEENEY gave instructions to the men on the motorboat on how to get to the rope ladder. Then he made Bantam climb back down.

"I had planned on using the rope that was inside the cave," he said to Bantam. "I put it in there for that purpose. You guys spoiled it. Then I was going to carry the painting out the basement door. But Farley's rope ladder simplifies everything. How come he's here this late at night? I told him yesterday that if I caught him in the cave again I'd skin him alive."

Soon the two men from the motorboat descended the ladder. One was tall, partially bald and wore a dark suit and necktie. The other was much shorter, broad-shouldered and wore a turtleneck sweater and a beret.

Sweeney put out his hand to the tall man and smiled. "Hello, Mr. Wales. You're right on time."

"I'm always punctual, Mr. Sweeney," replied Mr. Wales.

Had Sweeney forgotten what he'd said about identifying the men? He had addressed the man as Mr. Wales.

Mr. Wales' smile faded as he glanced at Bantam. "Who's the kid? What's he doing here? And what are you holding that gun for?"

"The kid's caught on," said Sweeney. "But don't worry. I'll tie him up and we'll be miles away from here before anybody will find him, if anybody ever will."

"Are you sure?"

"Yes, I'm sure. All right. You men wait here. I'll tie him up, and be right back with the painting."

Mr. Wales looked suspiciously at him.

"Put that gun away, Mr. Sweeney. I'm sure the three of us can handle a boy."

Sweeney hesitated. "The three of us?"

"We're going with you, Mr. Sweeney."

"You have the money?" Sweeney asked.

"It's on the boat. You'll get it. Now, let's get that painting."

Mr. Wales shoved Bantam ahead of them toward the dark depths of the cave and the men followed. Bantam saw his last chance of escaping vanish. The two men and Sweeney would pick up the painting and be on their way, and probably never be found again. The eccentric art collector would get his painting and Sweeney would get his fifty thousand dollars.

The only good that might come out of it would be Terry Lott's freedom. Maybe Mr. Torro, Old Farley, Kev and I will sit tied to

chairs in this old cave until we rot, thought Bantam. And when Aunt Janet and Uncle Dick find us, they will probably blame it all on me, because I had a reputation for getting into trouble. This time I was trying to help. But everything backfired. I have not only got myself into real trouble, but three other guys, too. If we're dead Aunt Janet and Uncle Dick will never know the truth.

"Hey! Where's that old buzzard?" cried Sweeney. "Where's Old Farley?"

They had walked as far as the bend in the cave. And no Old Farley!

"Old Farley? What are you talking about, Mr. Sweeney?" muttered Mr. Wales gruffly.

Sweeney didn't answer. He dashed past Bantam, leaving the boy and the men in pitch darkness. The men started running after him, bumping into Bantam as they swept by. One of them grabbed his arm and pulled him along.

"Come on! We're not going to take a chance letting you run back the other way!"

They reached Tony Torro and Kev. Both were still bound and gagged in their chairs.

"The old buzzard's gone," observed Sweeney. "He's probably gone to tell some- one we're here. Come on. I'll get the painting. You bring the kid. We can't leave him here now."

He picked up the painting from behind the bed, then started in a run toward the mouth of the cave. The stocky little man holding Bantam's arm seemed puzzled by what was going on, and relaxed his grip. Bantam, figuring it was now or never, yanked his arm free and rushed into the darkness toward where he guessed the base- ment door was.

"Hey! The kid's got away!" the man yelled.

"Get after him!" shouted Mr. Wales.

"You crazy?" cried the other. "This cave's pitch black!"

Bantam put his arms out in front of him to avoid getting hurt should he run into the cave's wall. He ran a short distance and bang! Right into a wall! Dazedly, he slowed his pace and felt his way along.

Cool air struck him full on the face. At the same time he saw a thin shaft of light, like a yellow glass about ten feet ahead of him. A second later the light broadened as the basement door swung open and the light shone full on him.

"Bantam!"

"Uncle Dick! They're in here! Two men! And Sweeney! He's got the painting! He's running out the other way with it and he's got a gun! Somebody's got to stop him, Uncle Dick! Somebody's got to—"

A comforting arm went around his shoulders. And then he saw that it wasn't Uncle Dick.

16

BANTAM!"

Somebody rushed past the person with the flashlight and pulled Bantam into his arms. "Bantam! Are you all right?"

This was Uncle Dick.

"Yes," whispered Bantam, trembling. "I'm all right. But somebody's got to stop—"

"Don't worry," interrupted Uncle Dick. "Two troopers are waiting at the other end of the cave. Sweeney will walk right into their arms." A warm chuckle bubbled from him. "Come on. You're soaking wet. You'd better get those clothes off right away and take a hot bath."

Bantam saw, then, that the person with the flashlight was Mr. Ward. He started to walk away with Uncle Dick and remembered something. "I didn't start any trouble, Uncle Dick. I was trying to help. . ."

"I know, Bantam. Mr. Farley told us. He thinks a lot of you. But not half as much as your Aunt Janet and I do."

Aunt Janet and Michelle and Terry Lott and a lot of other people were in the hall of Fugitive House, waiting for them. Aunt Janet's eyes were wet as she hugged Bantam. She seemed so happy to see him she couldn't utter a single word.

"He's soaking wet and chilled," said Uncle Dick. "He'd better get a hot bath right away before he catches pneumonia."

It was an hour later, while Bantam was lying on the bed, that Uncle Dick, Terry, Michelle, Nancy, Kev and Tony Torro came into the room. Aunt Janet was sitting on a chair, resting her eyes. Several times Bantam had thought that she had fallen asleep, but she hadn't.

125

"Well, the troopers have arrested Sweeney and the two agents," grinned Tony
Torro. "I feel sorry for Sweeney. I was
hoping he'd straighten out while he was
here."

"The police took the painting, too," said
Nancy breathlessly.

Bantam looked at Terry. Terry smiled.
"Nobody dreamed you boys would be in
the cave. No one's been in there for years."

"Except Mr. Farley," said a new voice.
"He goes there quite often."

The voice came from a person standing in
the doorway. It was Mr. Ward, with Old
Farley next to him, blinking and smiling
happily.

"Hello, Mr. Farley," grinned Bantam.
"Thanks for going after help. You saved
our lives."

Mr. Farley's eyes blinked even faster than
before. "Guess it was the first time I ever
helped anybody in my life," he confessed.

"This might be my first time, too," admitted Mr. Ward. "I'm giving Mr. Farley a
job. We need a good janitor in Fugitive

House, someone to keep the downstairs rooms cleaned." He looked at Old Farley. "Want a job, Mr. Farley?"

Mr. Farley nodded. "Nothing would please me more, Mr. Ward. Thank you. Thank you very much."

"Good. Tony, find a room for Mr. Farley. The man needs sleep." He looked at the old man. "Your pay will start immediately. But you don't start work until next week. Understand? Or you will be docked." With that he walked out of the room.

A few seconds later everybody in the room stared at each other and smiled. "There goes," said Tony Torro, "the nicest mean man I ever had the pleasure of knowing. Come on, Mr. Farley. Let's go. Good night, everybody."

A chorus of "Good-nights" followed them out of the room.

Kev came forward and placed a box on the bed. "Thought you might want this," he said.

Bantam stared. "My telescope! I'd forgotten about it! Say! That gives me an idea.

Want to come over tomorrow night and look at the stars with me, Kev? Can he, Aunt Janet? Uncle Dick?"

Aunt Janet and Uncle Dick smiled at each other. "He sure can," Aunt Janet said. "But not tomorrow night, dear. You're going to bed early tomorrow night. And I think it's time you went to sleep now, too."

He shrugged, and closed his eyes. Aunt Janet was right. He sure was tired.